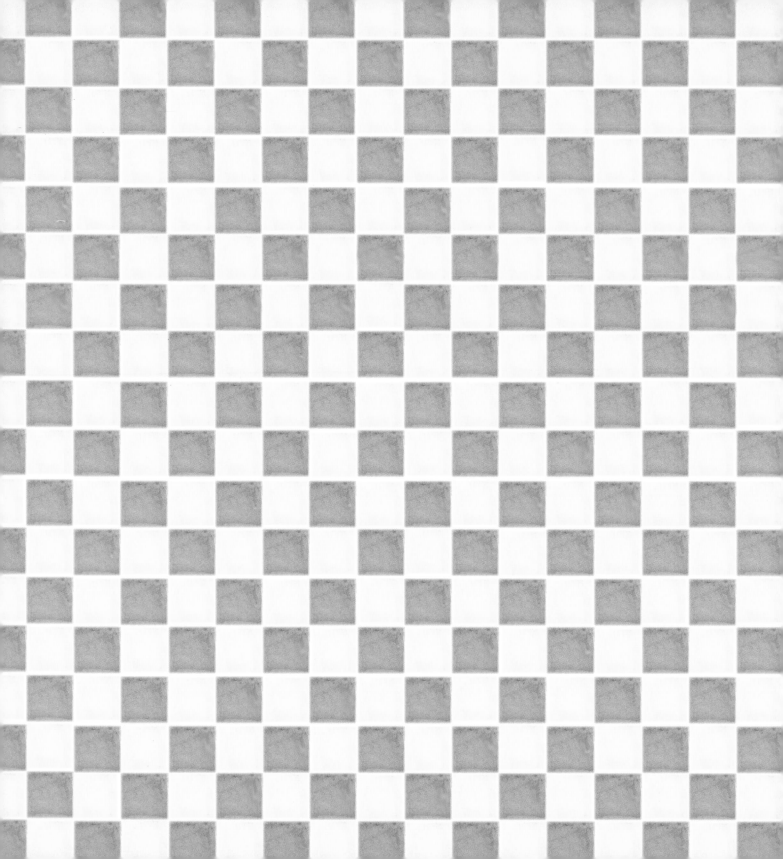

One Smart COOKIE

Bite-Size Lessons for the School Years and Beyond

written by
Amy Krouse Rosenthal

illustrated by
Jane Dyer & Brooke Dyer

HARPER
An Imprint of HarperCollins Publishers

Library of Congress Cataloging-in-Publication Data is available.
ISBN 978-0-06-142970-5 (trade bdg.) — ISBN 978-0-06-142971-2 (lib. bdg.)

Typography by Rachel Zegar
10 11 12 13 14 LP/LPR 10 9 8 7 6 5 4 3 2 1

First Edition

When cooking, it is important to keep safety in mind. Children should always ask
permission from an adult before cooking and should be supervised by an adult in
the kitchen at all times. The publisher and author disclaim any liability from any injury
that might result from the use, proper or improper, of the recipe contained in this book

For Ann and Paul
The smartest thing I've ever done
was being born your daughter
—A.K.R.

For Cecily, who is one smart cookie
Love from
—B.D. & J.D.

PROMPT means,

When it's time to make cookies,
we are here and ready on the dot!

ORGANIZED means
when everything is in its proper place,
it's so much easier to make the cookies.

UNORGANIZED means,

I put everything away quickly and without thinking last time and now I can't find what I need to make the cookies.

PREPARED means

looking at the cookie recipe ahead of time

to make sure you have everything you need.

UNPREPARED means

going ahead and making the batter only to realize halfway in that
you're out of chocolate chips and don't even have a baking sheet!

COMPROMISE means

she wanted to make really big cookies,

but he wanted to make teeny-tiny cookies,

so they thought about it together and
decided to make medium-size cookies.

EMPATHY means,

Your feelings somehow came into my feelings,
and it feels to me like you could use a cookie right now.

Thanks for understanding how I feel.

KINDNESS means,

Giving me your cookie was the nicest thing ever!

LISTENING means,

While you're explaining how to make the cookies,

I'm paying real close attention with my ears and even my eyes too.

CONTRIBUTE means

you don't just sit back while everyone else makes the cookies;

each of us is doing our part and adding something good.

Shall we call these chocolate "all-chip-in" cookies?

PROCRASTINATE means,

When they told us about the bake sale last week, I could have easily made one batch a day, but instead I kept putting it off, oh, I'll do it tomorrow, and now I have to bake a ton of batches all in one night.

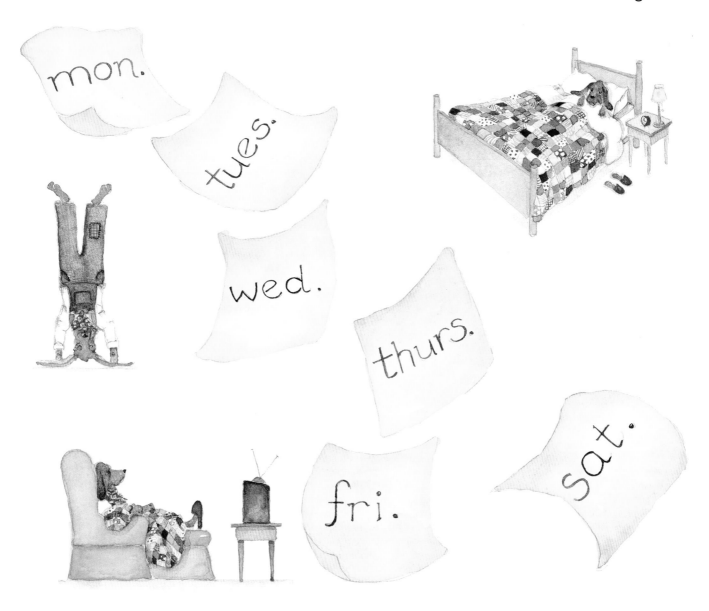

mon.

tues.

wed.

thurs.

fri.

sat.

DILIGENT means,

Without anyone reminding me, I came home each day
and worked really, really hard on the cookie project.

PERSEVERE means

we kept trying and trying and, even though this new recipe was super difficult, we never gave up, even when we ruined the cookies for the tenth time!

ARROGANT means,

Why is she acting like her cookies are
so much better than everyone else's?

HUMBLE means

she doesn't go around talking about how great her

cookies are; she just quietly does her thing.

These are the best cookies I've ever had!

Gosh, thank you so much!

PONDER means

concentrating and wondering and thinking carefully

about what kind of cookies to make for our friend.

DAYDREAM means,

I'm imagining all the wonderful things

I can do with cookies one day.

CREATIVE means

there are always fresh, new cookie ideas to be thought of!

DISHONESTY means,

Well, no one's around to see, so I'm taking the cookie.

INTEGRITY means,

It doesn't matter whether anyone sees or not.

I know inside myself that it's not my cookie to take.

I'm glad I left it there.

It makes me feel peaceful and whole.

CURIOUS means,

I want to know everything about these cookies!

Wow! There are so many different and wonderful kinds of cookies here! Which ones do you like the most? Who invents the recipes? And where do sprinkles come from, anyway?

INSPIRE means,

Seeing what you've done here fills me with energy and new thoughts and the desire to now try to see what I can do!

One Smart
COOKIE

INGREDIENTS

1 cup butter, softened

1 ½ cups sugar

2 eggs

1 ¼ teaspoons vanilla extract

2 ¼ cups all-purpose flour

1 teaspoon baking soda

1 teaspoon salt

12 rolls of Smarties candies (10 will probably do, but you might want some extras for snacking)

DIRECTIONS

Preheat oven to 315 ºF. In a medium bowl, mix together the flour, baking soda, and salt. In a large bowl, cream butter and sugar, then add the eggs one at a time, followed by the vanilla. Beat until light and fluffy. Gradually add the flour mixture using a wooden spoon or rubber spatula as the dough becomes thicker.

Drop by teaspoonfuls set 1½ inches apart onto ungreased baking sheets. Push 5 Smarties into each cookie. Bake for 20–25 minutes or until edges are light golden brown. Remove cookies with a metal spatula and cool on wire racks.

Makes about 40 cookies. Or save a sizable portion of the batter to make (you guessed it) One Smart Cookie.